Text and illustrations © 2014 Bayard Éditions
Translation © 2015 Christelle Morelli

Published in North America in 2016 by Owlkids Books Inc.

Published in France under the title *Blanche hait la nuit* in 2014 by Bayard Jeunesse

Owlkids Books acknowledges the financial support of the Canada Council for the Arts, the Ontario Arts Council, the Government of Canada through the Canada Book Fund (CBF) and the Government of Ontario through the Ontario Media Development Corporation's Book Initiative for our publishing activities.

Published in Canada by
Owlkids Books Inc.
10 Lower Spadina Avenue
Toronto, ON M5V 2Z2

Published in the United States by
Owlkids Books Inc.
1700 Fourth Street
Berkeley, CA 94710

Cataloguing data available from Library and Archives Canada

Library of Congress Control Number: 2015947464

ISBN 978-1-77147-158-9

Manufactured in Dongguan, China, in September 2015, by Toppan Leefung Packaging & Printing (Dongguan) Co., Ltd.
Job #BAYDC18

A   B   C   D   E   F

Publisher of Chirp, chickaDEE and OWL
www.owlkidsbooks.com | Owlkids Books is a division of   Bayard CANADA

Blanche Hates The Night

Written and illustrated by Sibylle Delacroix

Translated by Christelle Morelli

Owlkids Books

Good night, Blanche!

Every day ends the same.
Night always falls.

Blanche does not like the night.
Actually, Blanche hates the night!

So Blanche puts on a concert to chase away the moon and wake up the sun.

Do re mi...

The night is such a pain!

Do-on't want to sleep!

Everything is gray, and you're
not supposed to play.

To bed, my little songbird...

Sleep, sleep, birdie, sleep…

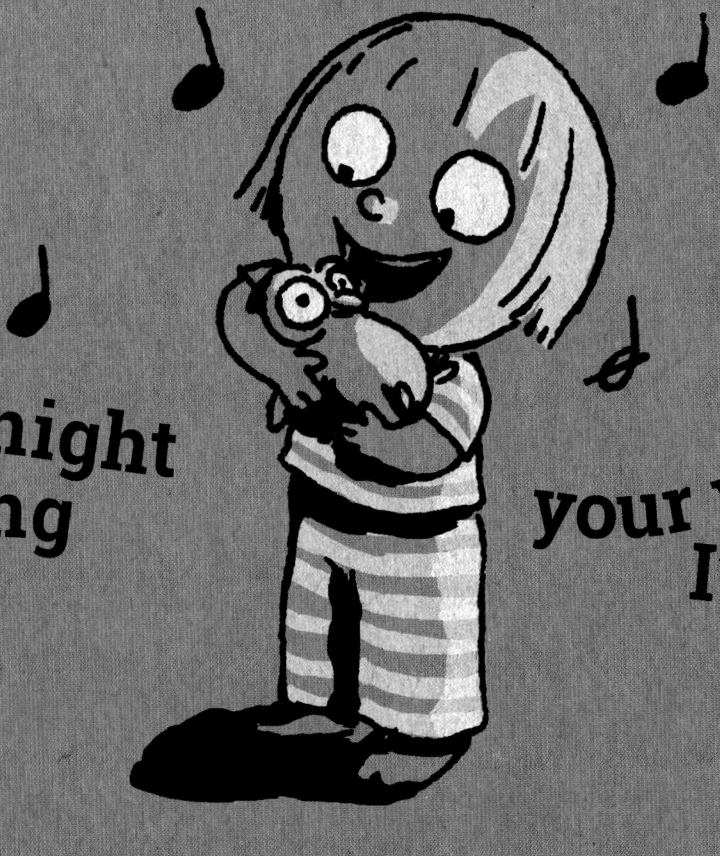

All night long your watch I'll keep!

The moon is only good for
hanging up your pajamas.

Blanche wants to horse
around!

Blanche! Back to bed!

And hop to it!

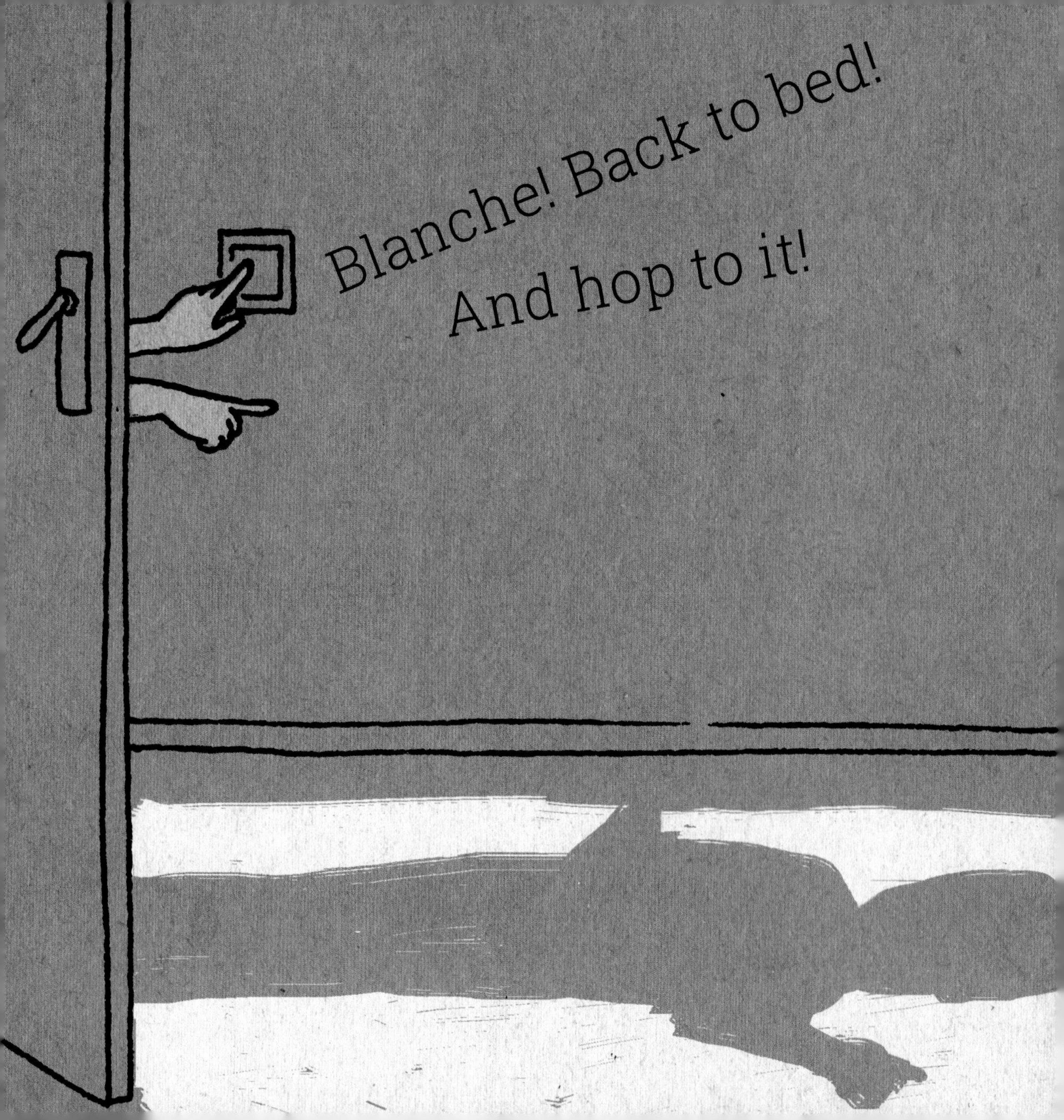

Oh yes! I can hop to it!

Hee, my bed is
my trampoline!

And it's my sleigh carrying me away, up so high where the sun never hides...

Up so high...
to the land
of midnight...

Zzzzzz...

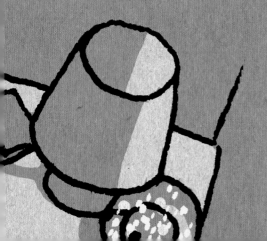

Good night,
Blanche...